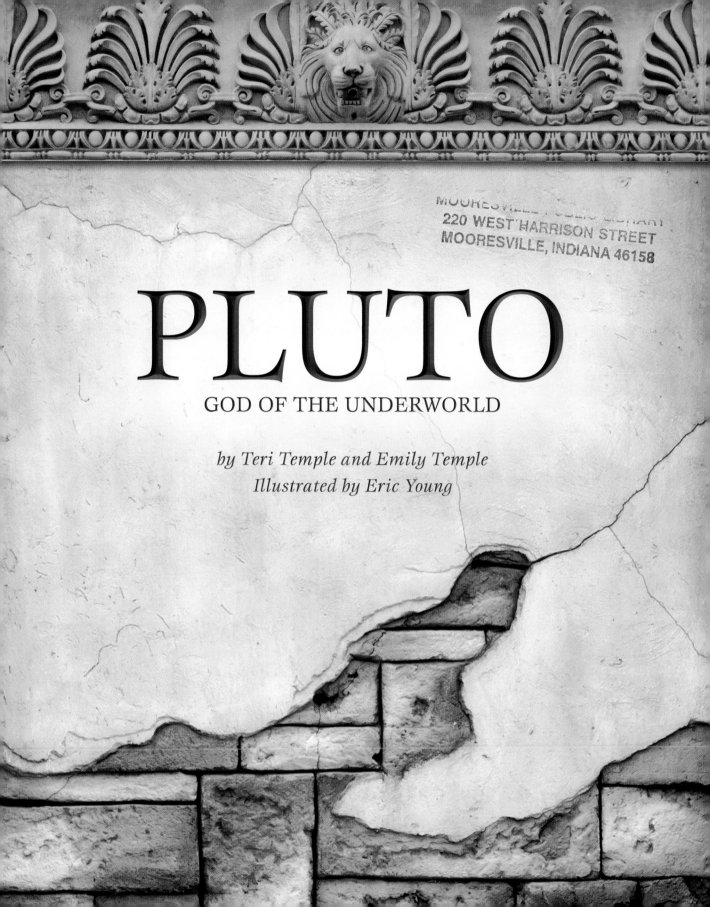

PLUTO

GOD OF THE UNDERWORLD

by Teri Temple and Emily Temple

Illustrated by Eric Young

Published by The Child's World®
1980 Lookout Drive • Mankato, MN 56003-1705
800-599-READ • www.childsworld.com

ACKNOWLEDGMENTS
The Child's World®: Mary Berendes, Publishing Director
Red Line Editorial: Editorial direction
The Design Lab: Design and production
Design elements ©: Banana Republic Images/Shutterstock Images; Shutterstock
Images; Anton Balazh/Shutterstock Images
Photographs ©: Viacheslav Lopatin/Shutterstock Images, 5; Joachim Patinir,
12; Christie's Images/Corbis, 14; Wenceslaus Hollar, 17; Vladimir Korosty-
shevskiy/Shutterstock Images, 24; Jacopo Caraglio, 28

ISBN 9781631437236
LCCN 2014945431

Printed in the United States of America
Mankato, MN
November, 2014
PA02241

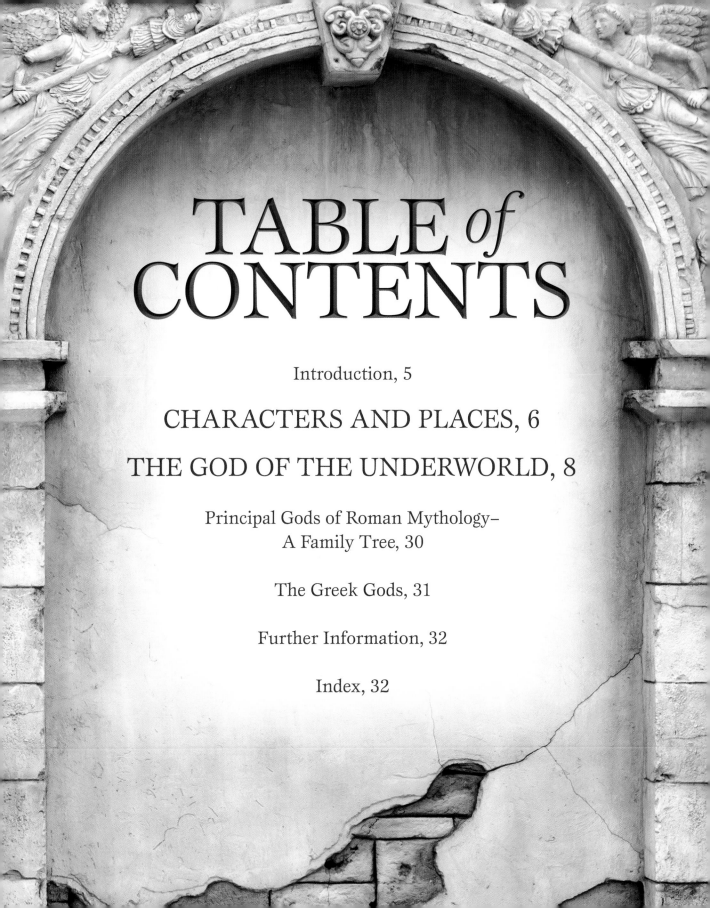

TABLE *of* CONTENTS

INTRODUCTION

In ancient times Romans believed in spirits or gods called numina. In Latin, *numina* means divine will or power. The Romans took part in religious rituals to please the gods. They felt the gods had powers that could make their lives better.

As the Roman government grew more powerful, its armies conquered many neighboring lands. Romans often adopted beliefs from these new cultures. They greatly admired the Greek arts and sciences. Gradually, the Romans combined the Greek myths and religion with their own. These stories shaped and influenced each part of a Roman citizen's daily life. Ancient Roman poets, such as Ovid and Virgil, wrote down these tales of wonder. Their writings became a part of Rome's great history. To the Romans, however, these stories were not just for entertainment. Roman mythology was their key to understanding the world.

ANCIENT ROMAN SOCIETIES
Ancient Roman society was divided into several groups. The patricians were the most powerful and wealthiest group. They often owned land and held power in the government. The plebeians worked for the patricians. Slaves were prisoners of war or children without parents. Some slaves were freed and enjoyed most of the rights of citizens.

CHARACTERS AND PLACES

ANCIENT ROME

ADRIATIC SEA

ROME

TYRRHENIAN SEA

N
W E
S

CERBERUS *(SUR-bur-uhs)*

Giant three-headed dog that guards the entrance to the underworld

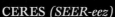

CERES *(SEER-eez)*

Goddess of the harvest; mother of Proserpine

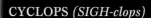

CYCLOPS *(SIGH-clops)*

One-eyed giants; children of Terra and Caelus

HECATONCHEIRES *(hek-a-TON-kear-eez)*

Monstrous creatures with 100 arms and 50 heads; children of Terra and Caelus

OPS *(ops)*

A Titaness; married to her brother Saturn; mother to the first six Olympic gods: Jupiter, Neptune, Pluto, Juno, Vesta, and Ceres

ORPHEUS *(OHR-fee-uhs)*

Mortal who traveled to the underworld to rescue his wife Eurydice

PIRITHOUS *(py-RITH-oh-uhs)*

Tried to kidnap Proserpine and ended up trapped in the underworld by Hades

PLUTO *(PLOO-toh)*

God of the underworld and death; son of Saturn and Ops, married to Proserpine

PROSERPINE *(PRAW-sur-pine)*

Daughter of the goddess Ceres; married to Pluto

SISYPHUS *(SIS-i-fuhs)*

Mortal whose punishment in the underworld was to forever push a boulder up a hill

OLYMPIAN GODS *(uh-LIM-pee-uhn)*: Ceres with daughter Proserpine, Mercury, Vulcan, Venus with son Cupid, Mars, Juno, Jupiter, Neptune, Minerva, Apollo, Diana, Bacchus, Vesta, and Pluto

TITANS *(TIE-tinz)*: The 12 children of Terra and Caelus; godlike giants who are said to represent the forces of nature

UNDERWORLD: The land of the dead; ruled over by the god of the dead, Pluto; must cross the River Styx to gain entrance

THE GOD OF THE UNDERWORLD

Pluto would become the god of death and lord of the underworld. Yet Pluto did not get off to a good start.

According to Roman mythology, there was only darkness at the beginning of time. Out of the darkness arose Mother Earth. She was also called Terra. She created the heavens and the god of the sky, called Caelus. Together, Terra and Caelus became the parents of a strong race of giants known as the Titans. The Titans represented the forces of nature. Without the Titans, there would be no stories of the Olympic gods.

Saturn, the youngest Titan, challenged his father, Caelus, to become ruler of the universe. The Titan fought his father in battle. Saturn won.

Saturn and his wife Ops went on to give birth to the first Olympic gods. But Saturn was nervous his children would defeat him, as he had defeated his own father. To protect himself, he swallowed each child after it was born.

Ops was sad without her children. She devised a plan to set them free. After giving birth to their sixth child, she hid him on an island. She gave Saturn a wrapped stone, pretending it was their child, Jupiter.

When Jupiter was grown, he returned to his parents with a potion for Saturn. It made Saturn throw up his first five children and the stone. Three sisters, Vesta, Ceres, Juno, and two brothers, Neptune and Pluto, emerged from his stomach. The six Olympic gods were free.

The Olympic gods wanted to defeat Saturn, but they needed help. Saturn had imprisoned his other children, the Cyclopes and the Hecatoncheires, in the underworld. Jupiter released them. These creatures would help the gods.

The Hecatoncheires were fearsome warriors. The Cyclopes built weapons. They were skilled blacksmiths. They made Pluto a helmet of darkness. This helmet allowed him to move invisibly among his enemies.

The battle between the Titans and the gods lasted ten years. Eventually the gods had the advantage. Pluto used his helmet to sneak into the Titans' camp. He stole all of their weapons. Then Jupiter blasted the Titans with a thunderbolt. The Cyclopes and Hecatoncheires threw boulders at the Titans.

The universe was nearly destroyed, so the Titans gave up. The world was finally at peace. After winning the battle, the Olympic gods built a new home on Mount Olympus. Now Jupiter was ruler. He divided the universe among his brothers. It was decided that Jupiter would be king of the gods and rule over the heavens. Neptune was made god of the seas. Pluto was granted reign over the underworld.

Ancient Romans thought the underworld lay deep beneath the secret places of the earth. Both ancient Greeks and Romans thought some of the afterlife was desolate and unhappy. As a result, the underworld was a dark and miserable place. But it suited Pluto perfectly.

THE RIVERS OF THE UNDERWORLD

Five rivers surrounded the underworld. The only poet who wrote clearly about the geography of the underworld was Virgil. He said a path led to where the Archeron River joined the Cocytus River. Three more rivers separated the underworld from the earth. These rivers were called the Phlegethon, the Lethe, and the River Styx.

In the underworld, Pluto lived in a palace. Only the spirits knew what the palace looked like. It was crowded with the souls of the dead and locked with a heavy gate. Cold meadows surrounded Pluto's home. The meadows were filled with strange pale flowers called asphodel.

Pluto's appearance matched his lonely home. Pluto was majestic, yet somber. He always carried a scepter to show he protected the underworld. Pluto was a stern god. Prayer and sacrifice had no effect on him. Pluto

was at home in the underworld, so he left the ruling of the universe and its problems to his siblings. He was not welcome on the earth or on Mount Olympus.

Though Pluto was a grim and somber god, he ruled the underworld well. He gave responsibilities to other beings. Then he made sure everyone did his or her job correctly. When a person died, his or her spirit traveled to the underworld for judgment. The journey to the underworld was not easy. First, the spirits had to cross the River Styx. They paid the ferryman, Charon, a coin for passage to the underworld. The spirits had to row themselves across the river. Charon steered the boat.

Once across, the spirits passed Cerberus. He was a three-headed, dragon-tailed dog that guarded the underworld entrance. Cerberus did not bother the spirits. His job was to keep out the living.

After passing Cerberus, the spirits reached a fork in the road.

JUDGES OF THE DEAD

Three judges decided the fate of the dead in the underworld. They were Rhadamanthus, Aecus, and Minos. These judges were sons of Jupiter. They were given immortality and the position as judge as a reward for creating law on the earth. Rhadamanthus was judge of the men from Asia. Aecus was guardian of the keys of the underworld. He was also judge of the men from Europe. Minos was the final vote. Some myths say there was a fourth judge named Tritolemus.

This is where they learned their fate. The three Judges of the Dead decided in which level of the underworld the spirit would live for eternity. Pluto did not help make these decisions.

The underworld had many different names in Roman mythology. These included Tartarus, Erebus, and Hades. Erebus was where the dead went first after they died. Erebus was a deeper level. It was the prison of the Titans. The underworld was often incorrectly called Hades. This was actually the name of a Greek god.

Pluto watched his helpers carefully. He wanted the underworld to work smoothly. The Judges of the Dead decided which level a spirit lived in. The first level was reserved for spirits of heroes. Spirits

THE FURIES
The Furies were serpent-haired daughters of Terra. They lived in the underworld, where they served as goddesses of revenge. Pluto had the Furies punish people. The Furies traveled to Earth to find mortals who had committed terrible crimes. They especially despised murderers. The Furies punished the wicked by driving them to madness.

lived here forever in paradise. Tartarus was home to the evildoers. Only the very wicked were sent to this level deep beneath the earth. Pluto sent the Furies to Tartarus to punish these souls. Most common souls went to a dull and dreary middle ground called Asphodel Fields.

Pluto wanted a bride to help him rule his kingdom. Even though the underworld was full of spirits and Pluto's attendants, the god was still lonely. Venus, the goddess of love, wanted him to find love as well. She told her son, Cupid, to shoot Pluto with an arrow to make him fall in love.

Pluto's sister, Ceres, had a daughter named Proserpine. She grew up on Mount Olympus. Several of the gods wanted to marry her because she was very beautiful. Even Pluto took notice. With the help of Cupid's arrow, Pluto fell in love with Proserpine. He wanted her as his bride. But Pluto knew Ceres would never let Proserpine go to the underworld. So Pluto crafted a plan to carry her off.

Proserpine was playing with water nymphs in a fountain in Sicily, Italy, near Mount Etna, a volcano. She set off to pick flowers in a nearby meadow. A dark chariot pulled by black horses charged out of the volcano. Pluto was holding the reins. He took Proserpine by surprise and dragged her screaming into the underworld.

When she discovered Proserpine was gone, Ceres was heartbroken. She wandered the earth in search of her beloved daughter. Ceres was the goddess of the harvest. She refused to let anything grow until she was reunited with her daughter. But Pluto refused to return Proserpine to the earth.

Ceres was so desperate she asked Jupiter for help. Jupiter knew he needed to fix the problem so plants would grow again. He sent Mercury to the underworld. Mercury was Jupiter's messenger. He found Proserpine in Pluto's gloomy palace. She was silent and somber, just like the god of the underworld. But when Proserpine saw Mercury she leapt to her feet. She was filled with hope that she would be reunited with her mother.

Pluto knew he had to follow Jupiter's command to send Proserpine back to the earth. Pluto offered Proserpine all the jewels and riches of the earth. He hoped to convince Proserpine into staying, but it did not work. To make sure she would remain, Pluto tricked her into eating a single pomegranate seed. According to the laws of the

Fates, anyone who ate food of the underworld could never permanently return to the land of the living. The Fates were three of Jupiter's daughters. These goddesses spun and cut the threads of life. This meant the Fates determined a person's path.

Even though Jupiter was ruler of the universe, he also had to follow the laws of the Fates. Jupiter, however, managed to work out a deal with the Fates. Proserpine was allowed to leave the underworld to spend four months on the earth with her mother. During that time, Ceres provided plenty of crops for the humans on the earth.

The other eight months Proserpine spent with Pluto in the underworld. She ruled with Pluto as the queen of the underworld. But Proserpine was not happy. Neither was her mother. Ceres's grief brought winter during the time Proserpine was not with her. The earth was barren and cold.

The rulings of the Fates were final. Humans were forced to patiently wait for spring each year. Proserpine's return brought about the springtime. By allowing Proserpine time with her mother, Pluto assured a harvest for the people of Earth. Because of this, Pluto came to be known as the god of the earth's fruitfulness, not just death.

Pluto was busy in the underworld with all of the problems death created. He worked all day and all night. Theseus and his friend Pirithous were two of the troublemakers Pluto had to deal with.

Pluto met Theseus and Pirithous when they traveled to the underworld to capture Proserpine. Pirithous wanted to marry the queen of the underworld. Theseus was helping to return a favor. They made their way to the underworld. They even got past Cerberus.

THESEUS
Theseus was a famous Greek hero from Athens. He was the son of Aegeus, king of Athens. Some myths say Theseus was the son of Neptune. Theseus played a role in many myths. He sailed with Jason and the Argonauts. He killed the Minotaur in the labyrinth on Crete. Theseus also kidnapped Helen from the Trojan War. And he was trapped in the underworld until Hercules set him free. Theseus continued to have adventures until his death.

The two mortals arrived in Pluto's palace and informed him they had come for Proserpine. Pluto laughed, amused by their bravery. He invited them to take a seat and discuss their plan, but he never intended to let them succeed.

When they sat down, Theseus and Pirithous were
suddenly unable to move or think. Pluto had tricked them
into sitting in the Chairs of Forgetfulness. Their minds
blank, the two remained stuck there for many years.

The Greek hero Hercules encountered Theseus and Pirithous while he was trying to complete one of his 12 labors. Hercules traveled to the underworld to convince Pluto to let him borrow Cerberus. Hercules was able to free Theseus but not Pirithous. Pluto would not let him take the man who had tried to kidnap his wife. Pirithous was forced to spend eternity in the underworld.

Another story follows Orpheus and his beloved wife, Eurydice. When Eurydice died from a snakebite, Orpheus was sad. He thought he could not live without her. He traveled to the underworld to win her back. Orpheus charmed his way into the underworld by using his musical talents. Once there, Proserpine allowed Orpheus and Eurydice to leave. Pluto had one rule, though. Orpheus could not look back at Eurydice until they were safely past the borders of the underworld.

Orpheus agreed. But as they neared the edge of the underworld, he turned to check on his wife. As soon as he looked back, Eurydice was whisked back to the underworld. Orpheus had to spend the rest of his life alone.

The name Pluto comes from the Greek word *ploutos*, which means wealth. The ancient Romans originally worshiped him as the god of all metals, jewels, and riches that lie under the earth. Pluto was considered similar to the Greek god of the underworld, Hades, and the Roman god Dis Pater.

Pluto ruled over all of the regions of the dead. Pluto never personally punished or tortured those found guilty of evildoings. He watched over the decisions made by the three judges. Pluto was the god of the dead, not the god of death. That privilege belonged to the Roman god Orcus.

Ancient Romans were convinced that just saying Pluto's name would attract his attention. The Romans did not know what Pluto would or would not do. During the festivals of the winter, animal sacrifices were made

DIS PATER AND PLUTO

Dis Pater was the Romans' original god of the underworld. In Latin, his name meant "rich father." Dis Pater was god of riches, fertile land, and mineral wealth from underground. Later, he was combined with the deities Pluto and Orcus. The ancient Roman people feared Dis Pater.

at the Roman Coliseum. In the middle of the arena, a fire was kept burning for sacrifices of animals with black fur. Pluto was also honored at funeral ceremonies. Slaves and servants dressed as Pluto or his ferryman, Charon.

Pluto was not considered one of the 12 major gods in the Roman Pantheon, but he still played an important role in the cycle of life. There would always be a need for the god of the dead.

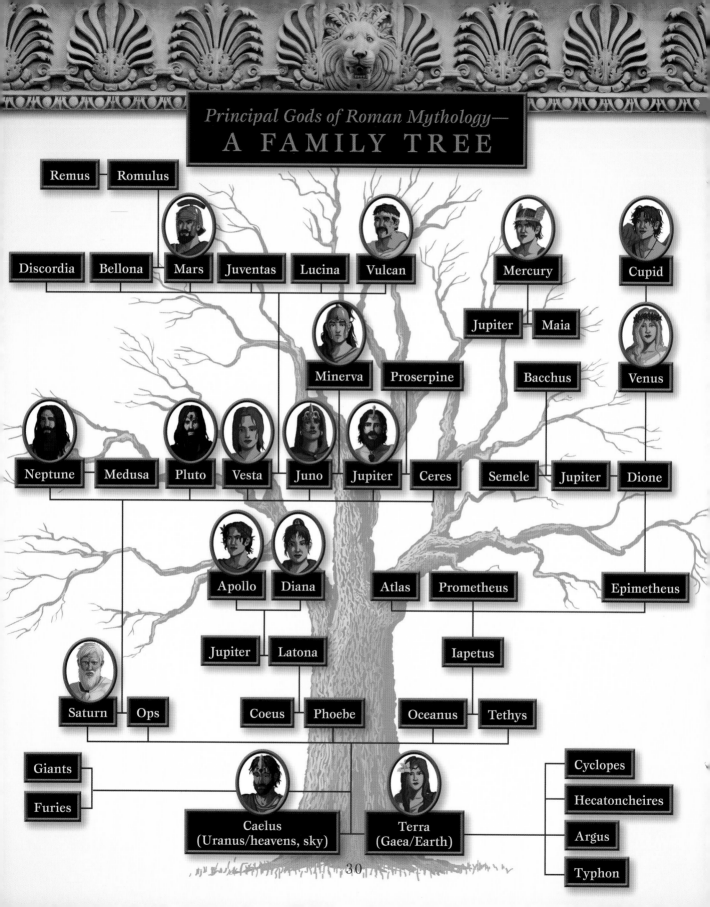

Principal Gods of Roman Mythology—
A FAMILY TREE

Remus — Romulus

Discordia — Bellona — Mars — Juventas — Lucina — Vulcan

Mercury

Cupid

Minerva — Proserpine

Jupiter — Maia

Bacchus

Venus

Neptune — Medusa — Pluto — Vesta — Juno — Jupiter — Ceres

Semele — Jupiter — Dione

Apollo — Diana

Atlas — Prometheus

Epimetheus

Jupiter — Latona

Iapetus

Saturn — Ops

Coeus — Phoebe

Oceanus — Tethys

Giants

Furies

Caelus
(Uranus/heavens, sky)

Terra
(Gaea/Earth)

Cyclopes

Hecatoncheires

Argus

Typhon

THE GREEK GODS

Ancient Greeks believed gods and goddesses ruled the world. The gods fell in love and struggled for power, but they never died. The ancient Greeks believed their gods were immortal. The Greek people worshiped the gods in temples. They felt the gods would protect and guide them. Over time, the Romans and many other cultures adopted the Greek myths as their own. While these other cultures changed the names of the gods, many of the stories remain the same.

SATURN: *Cronus*
God of Time and God of Sowing
Symbol: *Sickle or Scythe*

JUPITER: *Zeus*
King of the Gods, God of Sky, Rain, and Thunder
Symbols: *Thunderbolt, Eagle, and Oak Tree*

JUNO: *Hera*
Queen of the Gods, Goddess of Marriage,
  Pregnancy, and Childbirth
Symbols: *Peacock, Cow, and Diadem*
  (Diamond Crown)

NEPTUNE: *Poseidon*
God of the Sea
Symbols: *Trident, Horse, and Dolphin*

PLUTO: *Hades*
God of the Underworld
Symbols: *Invisibility Helmet and Pomegranate*

MINERVA: *Athena*
Goddess of Wisdom, War, and Arts and Crafts
Symbols: *Owl, Shield, Loom, and Olive Tree*

MARS: *Ares*
God of War
Symbols: *Wild Boar, Vulture, and Dog*

DIANA: *Artemis*
Goddess of the Moon and Hunt
Symbols: *Deer, Moon, and Silver Bow and Arrows*

APOLLO: *Apollo*
God of the Sun, Music, Healing, and Prophecy
Symbols: *Laurel Tree, Lyre, Bow, and Raven*

VENUS: *Aphrodite*
Goddess of Love and Beauty
Symbols: *Dove, Swan, and Rose*

CUPID: *Eros*
God of Love
Symbols: *Bow and Arrows*

MERCURY: *Hermes*
Messenger to the Gods, God of Travelers and Trade
Symbols: *Crane, Caduceus, Winged Sandals,*
  and Helmet

FURTHER INFORMATION

BOOKS

Johnson, Robin. *Understanding Roman Myths*. New York: Crabtree Publishing, 2012.

Temple, Teri. *Hades: God of the Underworld*. Mankato, MN: Child's World, 2013.

WEB SITES

Visit our Web site for links about Pluto: *childsworld.com/links*

*Note to Parents, Teachers, and Librarians: We routinely verify our Web links to make sure
they are safe and active sites. So encourage your readers to check them out!*

INDEX